This book belongs to

....

This is a Parragon Publishing book
First published in 2007

Parragon Publishing
Queen Street House
4 Queen Street
Bath BA1 1HE, UK

ISBN 978-1-4054-9109-9
Printed in China

Little Women

Written by Louisa May Alcott
Retold by Rachel Elliot
Illustrated by Elena Selivanova

Meg, Jo, Beth, and Amy March lived in a little house with their mother. Their father was far away, where the fighting was. They didn't have much money, but they were always thinking up new games and having fun.

Meg worked as a governess, but she didn't like it very much.

Jo dreamed of being a famous writer one day. She tried to be good, but she was always losing her temper and making mistakes. How she wished that she had been a boy!

Beth was very shy and gentle.
She could play the piano and
she loved music.

Amy was just
a little bit
vain, and she
loved drawing
and painting.

Their mother, who they called Marmee, was
very kind. She gave food and clothes to a family
called the Hummels, who were very poor.

One day, Jo and Meg were invited to a Christmas party. They had only their old dresses to wear.

"Mine has a burn at the back!" exclaimed Jo. "What shall I do?"

"Just sit down as much as you can," said Meg. "And don't stand like a boy, or use slang words!"

"I'll be as prim as I can," Jo laughed.

Meg had fun at the party, but Jo was bored. She didn't like gossiping with the other girls. Then she met a boy with curly black hair and twinkling eyes. His name was Theodore Laurence.

"Call me Laurie," he said. "I don't like my first name."

"I hate my name, too," said Jo. "I wish everyone would say Jo, instead of Josephine."
Laurie told Jo all about the places he had traveled to, and they made each other laugh a lot. Jo decided that the party wasn't so bad after all!

Laurie lived with his grandfather, Mr. Laurence, and his tutor, Mr. Brooke. He became good friends with all the March girls. One day, Jo went to see a show with Laurie, but she wouldn't take Amy.
So Amy burnt Jo's writing book!
All her stories were gone forever.
"I'll never forgive you as long as I live!" Jo shouted.

The next day, Jo and Laurie went skating on the frozen river. Amy followed them, but Jo ignored her. Then CRASH! The ice broke and Amy fell into the icy water!

Laurie and Jo raced across the ice. They pulled Amy out of the water and took her home. Amy was safe, but Jo felt very guilty.

"It's my dreadful temper!" she cried. "I try to cure it, and then it breaks out worse than ever!"

"Don't cry," said Marmee, kindly. "Keep trying, and one day you will learn how to control it."

Early that spring, Meg went to stay with her friend Annie Moffat. Her sisters helped her pack.

"Two weeks of fun, you lucky thing!" smiled Jo.

"And such lovely weather!" Beth added happily.

"I will tell you all about it when I get back," Meg promised.

Meg was very jealous of Annie Moffat's beautiful clothes. One evening, the Moffats held a party. Annie lent Meg a sky-blue dress, with jewelry and feathers. She lent her lipstick and powder. But instead of feeling grown up, Meg felt like a little doll. She wished that she had worn her simple, white dress.

When she got home, she told Marmee all about it.

"I know I was silly," she said. "But it was nice to be praised and admired."

"Learn to know the praise that is worth having," said Marmee. "Wise people will praise you for being good, not just for being pretty." Meg hugged her. She felt very glad that she could talk to her mother about anything.

Summer was coming, and the girls played lots of new games now that the days were so long. They made up a secret society and wrote a newspaper for it every week. They played at housekeeping, and Jo even tried to cook dinner. Jo was trying hard to control her temper. It was difficult, but she was learning, and Marmee was very proud of her.

The girls spent long summer days with Laurie, having picnics, reading to each other, and rowing on the river. They met Mr. Brooke, Laurie's tutor, and liked him very much. He and Meg spent lots of time together, talking about their hopes and dreams.

"As soon as Laurie has gone to college, I shall become a soldier," Mr. Brooke said. "I am needed."

"It is hard for the mothers and sisters who stay at home," said Meg. She thought about her father, at war far away. They missed him very much.

When the fall came, Jo spent a lot of time in the attic, writing. She scribbled away until the last page was filled.

"There, I've done my best!" she exclaimed. She tied her work up with a red ribbon and went into town.

A few days later, Jo read a story out of the newspaper to her sisters. They liked it very much.

"Who wrote it?" asked Beth.

"I did!" Jo exclaimed. She had taken her story to the newspaper and they had liked it enough to print it! Everyone was very excited, but nobody was happier than Jo. This was her first step toward her dream!

One day, Laurie told Jo a secret that made her very angry.

"I know where Meg's lost glove is," he said. "I saw it in Mr. Brooke's pocket. He has kept it all this time. Isn't that romantic?"

"No," said Jo, furiously. "It's ridiculous!"
Jo didn't want anyone to take her sister away.

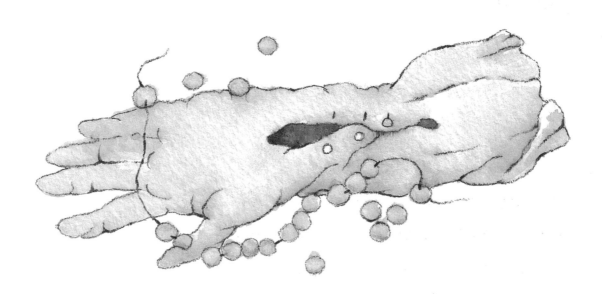

One frosty winter's day, a terrible telegram arrived.

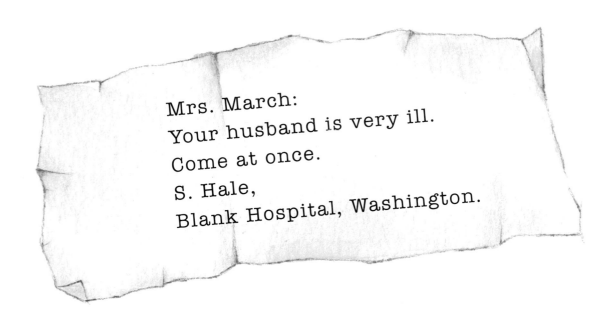

Mrs. March:
Your husband is very ill.
Come at once.
S. Hale,
Blank Hospital, Washington.

Mrs. March went as white as a sheet.

"I shall go today," she said, "but it may be too late!"
Mr. Brooke said that he would escort Marmee to Washington.
But Jo knew that her mother would need money to pay for
the journey. She hurried out and was gone for a long time.

When Jo came back, she had a very strange look on her face. She gave twenty-five dollars to her mother.

"That's my bit toward bringing Father home!" she said.

"My dear, where did you get it?" gasped Marmee.

"I only sold what was my own," said Jo. She took off her bonnet, and everyone gave a cry. She had sold her hair!

"Your one beauty!" Amy exclaimed.

But Marmee just gave Jo a loving look that warmed her heart.

It was very hard to watch Marmee leave, but the girls tried to be strong while she was away. After a few days, Marmee sent a letter. The doctors were sure that Father was going to get well, and the girls were filled with relief.

At first, they all worked hard around the house. But after a while, only little Beth did all her chores faithfully every day. And only Beth remembered to visit the Hummels, the poor family that Marmee cared for.

"Jo, I wish you'd go and see the Hummels," said Beth, one afternoon. "The baby is sick, and I don't know what to do for it."

"Too stormy for me with my cold," Jo said. So Beth put on her hood and went out into the chilly air.

It was late when she came back. Jo found her in Marmee's room, crying.

"What's the matter?" exclaimed Jo.

"Oh, Jo, the baby's dead!" sobbed Beth. "It was scarlet fever!"

"I ought to have gone!" cried Jo. "If you get sick, I'll never forgive myself!"

But Beth was sick. Jo nursed her day and night. The fever
made Beth delirious, and her throat was so swollen that
she couldn't speak. The days seemed very dark and long.
The milkman, baker, grocer, and butcher asked how she was.
All the neighbors sent little gifts. Shy little Beth had made
lots of friends.

Beth lay hour after hour, tossing back and forth. Jo never left her side. The doctor shook his head.

"If Mrs. March can leave her husband, she'd better be sent for," he said.

Jo rushed out to send a telegram to her mother.

All day long the snow fell and the bitter wind raged.

"I wish I had no heart, it aches so," sighed Meg.

At last, early the next morning, Jo saw the pain leave Beth's face. The fever had gone!

Suddenly they heard a carriage arrive, and then a familiar voice. Marmee was home!

It was wonderful to have Marmee back. Now that Beth was
not in danger, Jo told her mother about Mr. Brooke taking
Meg's glove.

"Isn't it dreadful?" she exclaimed.

"John Brooke is a very good, kind man," said Marmee.
"He has told your father and me that he loves Meg, and he
wants to marry her."
Jo felt unhappy. She didn't want anyone to take Meg away,
however good they were!

On Christmas Day, Beth felt much better. Their friends were there too, and they had a very merry time.

"If only Father was here, I would be completely happy," said Beth

Just then, Laurie popped his head around the door.

"Here's another Christmas present for the March family," he said.

Behind him was someone they had been longing to see for more than a year.

"FATHER!" they cried. Everyone rushed to hug and kiss him.

It was a perfect Christmas!

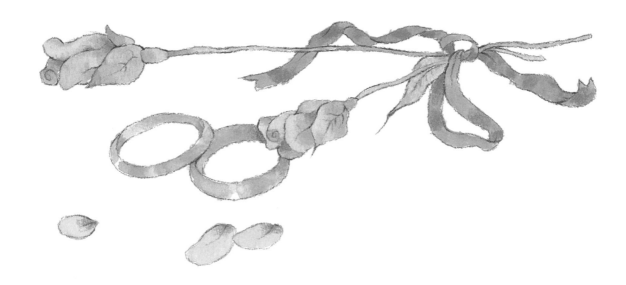

John Brooke did ask Meg to marry him, and she said yes.
At first, Jo was jealous and upset, but then Laurie came to talk to her.

"You can't know how hard it is for me to give up Meg," she said, and
her voice quivered. "I've lost my dearest friend."

"You've got me, Jo," said Laurie. "Don't be sad. Meg is happy."
Jo knew that Laurie was right. How could she be angry with Mr. Brooke
for making her sister so happy?

That evening in the parlor, Jo looked around at her family.
Father and Marmee were talking quietly together. Beth was talking
happily to old Mr. Laurence. Amy was drawing Meg and Mr. Brooke.

"Don't you wish that we could look forward and see where we
shall all be in three years?" asked Laurie.
Jo smiled at him.

"I think not," she said. "I don't believe we could be much happier
than we are right now!"